This edition published by Parragon Books Ltd in 2014 and distributed by

Parragon Inc
440 Park Avenue South, 13th Floor
New York, NY 10016
www.parragon.com
Copyright © Parragon Books Ltd 2014

Written by Rachael Duckett, Illustrations and sets created by Harriet Muncaster
Typeset in Bookeyed Martin © Font Diner—www.fontdiner.com

ISBN 978-1-4723-4925-5
Printed in China

Get a FREE eBook!

Use code GBE415 at www.glitterbelle.com

Limited Number Available. Exp Aug 2015

Glitterbelle™
The Sparkliest
Princess Ever!

By Rachael Duckett and

Harriet Muncaster

Bath • New York • Cologne • Melbourne • Delhi
Hong Kong • Shenzhen • Singapore • Amsterdam

Once upon our time, there lived the most glittery and sparkle-tastic princess, named Glitterbelle.

Glitterbelle loved everything sparkly, shimmery, and purple. She also loved animals, playing with her friends, and climbing trees. But there was something that Glitterbelle definitely did not love—and that was PEAS!

At dinner, even if the peas had been beautifully laid out on her plate, Glitterbelle would not touch them.

"Darling, won't you just try them?" asked her mom, Queen Lizzie.

"But I hate peas!" said Glitterbelle. "They're squishy, gross, and ... green!" She wrinkled her nose and looked at her little dog, Bob, who did the same.

"How do you know you don't like peas if you've never tried them?" asked her dad, King Alfie. "We love them. In fact, we owe our kingdom to peas."

"It's thanks to peas that your great-great-great-great-grandpapa found your great-great-great-great-grandma!" added the Queen. "Remember the famous fairy tale?"

"You mean the one where the Princess had a terrible night's sleep because she could feel one tiny pea under twenty mattresses?" said Glitterbelle. "The one where the pea proved that she was a REAL princess? The one where they got married in beautiful sparkly outfits and lived happily ever after?"

"That's the one!" grinned King Alfie. "The wedding was dazzling. And we still have that famous pea. It's a family treasure that will be yours one day!"

He went to the cabinet of royal treasures and took out a diamond-covered box. Inside, on the plushest, most silky satin pillow was ... a shriveled, old pea.

"Gross!" said Glitterbelle.

King Alfie laughed. "This pea is a bit ancient, but the ones we have for dinner are lovely and fresh. All princesses love peas—won't you try just one?"

Glitterbelle returned to the dining room table. She stared doubtfully at the peas on her plate.

"I must be the first princess EVER who doesn't like peas!" she thought.

Just then, Glitterbelle's best friends, Dazzlina and Angel, stopped by. The King and Queen left the three girls to talk together. As soon as they had gone, Glitterbelle sighed.

"What's the matter, Glitterbelle?" asked Angel.

"My mom and dad say that princesses love peas, but I hate them!" said Glitterbelle.

"I love peas!" cried Dazzlina, who was a witch. "They're green, just like my favorite things—frogs, grasshoppers, and Kat's eyes!"

"Meow," agreed Kat the Cat, appearing like magic next to Dazzlina.

"Angel loves peas too," said Dazzlina. "Don't you, Angel?"

"All ballerinas adore them," nodded Angel. "They're small, sweet, and round, like the buns in our hair ... and they're SO green, just like my gecko, George!"

Glitterbelle shook her head. Why didn't ANYONE understand?

"Don't worry, I have an idea," said Dazzlina, with a twinkle in her eye. She waved her magic wand in the air.

"Little plate of lovely peas,
Turn to popcorn, if you please!"

"Amazing!" said Angel.

"Poptabulous!" laughed Glitterbelle.

They each took a handful of popcorn and ran into the palace gardens to play on their scooters.

The girls raced around the gardens, around the fountain, and through an archway sparkling with string lights. Glitterbelle skidded to a stop in front of her favorite tree.

"Let's climb. I'll race you to the top!" she shouted.

Of course Glitterbelle won. She was amazing at climbing trees—even in a tiara!

"I love it up here," said Glitterbelle. "You can see all the way down into our town. Look, Angel, there's your house!"

"And there's mine!" cried Dazzlina.

"There's our school!" said Angel.

Glitterbelle looked thoughtful. She turned to her friends and asked, "Can I tell you a secret?"

Dazzlina and Angel nodded eagerly.

"Even though I'm a princess, one day I'd like to be our town vet and look after all the sick animals!" said Glitterbelle.

Angel gasped. "Wow, Glitterbelle, that's a great idea! You'd be an amazing vet."

Bob the Dog barked excitedly in agreement.

"But what about being a princess?" said Angel.

"You know, sometimes you don't act like a princess at all," giggled Dazzlina. "Princesses usually ride around in carriages, not on scooters!"

"And whoever heard of a princess who climbs trees and totally hates peas?" added Angel.

"Maybe you're right," said Glitterbelle, thinking of all the fairy-tale princesses she'd read about. "Maybe I'm not a real princess at all!"

"Oh, we didn't mean that!" said Angel. "We were only teasing."

"No, it's true," said Glitterbelle. "I AM different to the fairy-tale kind of princess. But anything they can do, I can do too!"

Glitterbelle scrambled down from the tree, followed by her two friends. She straightened her tiara and marched up to the well, where a frog was sitting quietly in the shade.

"What are you doing, Glitterbelle?" asked Dazzlina.

Glitterbelle shuddered. Frogs were SO slimy, but fairy-tale princesses were always kissing them and turning them into handsome princes. "Just watch this!" she said.

Glitterbelle gently picked up the frog, closed her eyes, and kissed it.

"Yucky!" said Angel.

"Awesome!" said Dazzlina, who loved frogs.

"Ribbit!" croaked the surprised frog, jumping out of Glitterbelle's hands.
It had clearly NOT turned into a handsome prince.

The frog blinked, then it jumped down the well, splashing water all over
Glitterbelle. She stumbled back from the well, tearing her dress and
losing a shoe on the path behind her.

"I really need a fairy godmother," said Glitterbelle. "Just look
at my clothes!"

"Oh, Glitterbelle," said Angel. "We love you whether you're
a fairy-tale princess or a scruffy, tree-climbing one!"

"Thanks, Angel," said Glitterbelle. "But I don't feel very princessy just
now." She picked up her shoe and walked back to the palace.

"Glitterbelle, are you all right?" asked Queen Lizzie when she
saw Glitterbelle. "Whatever happened?"

"I was trying to prove that I could be a fairy-tale princess," cried Glitterbelle, "but it all went wrong! I'm not a proper princess at all, am I?"

"Oh, Glitterbelle," said Queen Lizzie, "you're a proper princess, just by being you!" She hugged Glitterbelle and said, "It will all seem better in the morning, I promise."

While Glitterbelle went off for a bath, Queen Lizzie wondered how to prove to Glitterbelle that she was a proper princess. Then she had a wonderful idea.

Smiling, she went quietly upstairs to Glitterbelle's room and popped something small, round, and green under her mattress!

Before bed, Glitterbelle soaked in a bath full of bubbles, daydreaming about princesses in carriages, princesses turning frogs into handsome princes, princesses climbing trees, and vets wearing sparkly princess tiaras.

Glitterbelle was very sleepy, but when she finally went to bed, she just could not get comfortable. She tossed and she turned, and she barely slept a wink the whole night through!

The next morning, she woke up aching all over. It was almost as if she had slept on the floor, rather than on a lovely, fluffy mattress.

Then, as she climbed out of bed, a small green pea rolled out from under the mattress. Glitterbelle picked it up and knew at once why she hadn't been able to sleep.

The tiny pea proved that she was a fairy-tale princess too, just like her great-great-great-great-grandma!